for Josh
Merry (

Grubson Pug's
Christmas Voyage

By Jane-Anne Hodgson
Illustrations by Sam Hodgson

Whistling Cat Books

Grubson Pug's Christmas Voyage

Published by Whistling Cat Books
www.whistlingcatbooks.com

PO Box 385, Burford, OX18 9DH

Copyright © Jane-Anne Hodgson 2011

Hardback ISBN 978-1-908607-00-3
Paperback ISBN 978-1-908607-01-0

Designed and typeset by HL Studios, Witney, Oxfordshire.
Printed and bound by Information Press Limited, Eynsham, Oxfordshire.

FSC
www.fsc.org
MIX
Paper from
responsible sources
FSC® C013262

For Captain
My darling Dad

Who told me stories on dark and stormy nights when I couldn't sleep, made every childhood Christmas magical and who has always kept a light burning in the window. Safe haven.

Grubson Pug's Christmas Voyage

Captain John Selby

In the book, it is Captain John Selby who tells the story, as it was told to him one night by Grubson. The real Captain Selby was one of Jane's ancestors and he was a pirate – a good pirate! Registered to Queen Elizabeth I, he was licensed to attack and raid the Spanish Armada.

Jane remembers visiting the family home of Captain Selby's descendants when she was a small child. There was a retired parrot in the parlour, a grand piano in the drawing room, a cat who kept to the shadows and a collection of musical aunts with tales to tell. Jane has clear memories of sitting on her grandfather's knee, too close to the fireside, listening to his seafaring stories. A bit like Henri!

Jane-Anne Hodgson

A former English teacher and Creative Writing tutor, Jane lives in landlocked Oxfordshire. She often runs away to Pembrokeshire where she spent many summers as a child and where she now writes. The castles, old harbour towns, hidden beaches and remote islands remain magical to her. Those who know Tenby may recognise thinly-disguised elements of St Benfro and Monastery Island.

Jane has three nephews who have been her inspiration to tell stories over many years. All four of them would stay up late into the night spinning tales of adventure, naughtiness and magic. The legacy of these years is an attic full of stories which have yet to see the light of day. Grubson Pug's Christmas Voyage is Jane's first published children's book.

Sammy Jim!
One of these lively nephews is Sammy Jim – more properly known as Sam Hodgson.

Now a full-time art student, Sam is far too old to indulge in stories with his aunt. However, he was the natural choice as illustrator for this book. Having read the story, he knew exactly how to transfer the characters from the written word to pictures.

The illustrations in this book are all hand-drawn using pen and ink, which gives them a traditional feel with some quirky details.

This is Sam's first illustrative commission. He and Jane hope it is to be the first of many illustrated books.

Contents

Foreword

Y ou'd like Grubson Pug if you met him.
He's a sea-dog and is the captain of his own
ship – which is a very exciting and sometimes very
dangerous thing to be.

Grubson lives in St Benfro, a seaside town in the west
of Wales. He is partly French and partly Pug and a little
bit Welsh. Many years ago, his great-great-great-great-great
grandfather sailed from St Malo in France to St Benfro, fell
in love with the harbour-master's daughter and married
her. They lived in a tall, white-washed house overlooking the
harbour and generations of Grubsons have lived in this house
ever since.

Grubson lives there now with his wife Adele (who is French) and their four children. From the window of Grubson's study, he can see the harbour of St Benfro and has a lovely view of his own ship, a very ancient vessel called The Beagle. The Beagle herself (ships are always female) has a very interesting history having sailed the high seas all around the world many times over with her previous owners and if ships could speak ... but that's another story.

One stormy and moonless night, I met Grubson in The Three Buccaneers in St Benfro. We spent the evening cosily sitting too close to the fireside telling stories about our voyages, whilst the storm raged outside.

This is one of Grubson's stories and it's about Christmas, so I thought you'd like to hear it.

Captain John Selby

Grubson Pug's Christmas Voyage

Foreword

Grubson Pug's Christmas Voyage

Chapter One

Christmas Is Coming

One dark night – the fifth of December to be exact – Grubson looked up from his newspaper and studied the faces of his family gathered around the long kitchen table.

Mrs Grubson was pouting, peering through a magnifying glass at a recipe book.

Fabrice, having had seconds (and thirds) of their mackerel supper, was shifting about on his seat uncomfortably. He'd been complaining about blisters in difficult places due to his (stupid) bicycle saddle. He was now picking silver paper off a half-melted chocolate bar which he'd found in his pocket. He was dribbling in anticipation of the taste when he finally got past the foil.

Clementina was trimming her claws, frowning as she inspected each one; they clicked on the piano keys and annoyed her, which she said they wouldn't if she had a proper piano. Tunelessly humming to herself, she concentrated on getting the clippers onto each claw, her tongue stuck out looking like a little piece of ham.

Bella was looking at a fashion magazine, closely examining every item of clothing. She sighed at the lace collars and the pearl buttons, exclaiming to herself at the velvet winter cloaks and high boots. Her head was full of desperate thoughts.

'If only I had these beautiful clothes, I would be pretty and admired and popular,' she muttered to herself. Her face was scrunched up in a frenzy of envious, angry jealousy, her pearly white teeth like vicious fangs beneath her scowling lips.

Henri was examining a new sea chart which he had found rolled under a desk; he was tracking a make-believe voyage from St Benfro to New Guinea, imagining how he would outrun the pirates and find all their buried treasure.

Henri hoped to be the next Grubson to be a sailor but whenever he mentioned this, his mother went silent and his siblings laughed.

Perhaps an extra word or two about Henri is needed here.

He was really quite different from the rest of the family.

Laughed at by his brother and sisters and tutted at by his mother, he was the weeniest and wheeziest of the family. The runt.

Small, sensitive and a tiny bit afraid of anything involving a ball, he was left out of all the games. Sitting on his own near the flower beds, he would watch other children playing in the park but he wasn't ever allowed to join in.

He was the last to be fed around the table in the evening, struggling to chew and swallow the stringy bits of meat which had been left for him at the bottom of the pot. As time went by he found himself alone much of the time, with no one to talk to and nothing to do except read the tide tables and look at the maritime charts which were rolled up in his father's study.

When Grubson was away at sea, Henri spent hours on his own learning how to plan voyages according to the tides and the currents. He used a big blotchy pen to draw his imaginary journeys on the colourful charts. The hours he spent learning by himself meant that he soon became very clever at picking a careful course to avoid hidden rocks and raised sandbanks.

Henri had never been on a ship but he always waved to Grubson from the harbour when The Beagle set off on a voyage. He would wave and wave (and wave) until he was only waving at a tiny speck.

He would sit on the wall until well after sunset, staring in the direction of The Beagle until finally he would have one last big squeezy stare at the speck, just to check that it had gone and then trot slowly home.

Brings a lump to your throat doesn't it? Anyway, back to Grubson's story . . .

Grubson looked up from his newspaper:

'Here we are at the beginning of December. I have no more voyages to make this year, so The Beagle will stay in the harbour and I can spend Christmas on dry land. I'll be home for Christmas for the first time in many years! We'll have a tree lit with candles and decorated with sea shells. We'll sing carols around the piano and play games and tell stories. I'm already starting to feel excited – what about you?'

No one said anything. Not a word.

The sound of scrambling claws broke the silence as Henri slid down from his stool, scampered across the polished wood floor and scrabbled up onto Grubson's lap. Holding Grubson's tired old face in his tiny paws, Henri grinned from ear to ear and shouted.

'That is wonderful news Papa! You will be here with your stories and games and we can all have fun together!' Henri grinned widely down the table, looking first at his mother and then from face to face of his siblings.

Clementina mumbled, 'And what about presents?'

Grubson, who hadn't quite heard, leaned forward and lifted an ear in her direction, 'What was that Clementina?' he asked.

'She SAID . . .' burst out Bella loudly. 'She said what about our presents? You didn't mention those and after all, that's what Christmas is for! It's for presents and for children. It's for presents FOR children. And you forgot to say that!'

'I see,' said Grubson sitting back again, stroking the silky fur just behind Henri's right ear.

He felt a tiny bit shocked. Of course he hadn't forgotten about presents, but those were supposed to be secrets and surprises.

'Grubson, I think you should ask the children what they want because if you put your mind to it – *now* – you should have time to do something about it!' said Adele.

'I see,' said Grubson again. 'You're right my darling – as ever. And so, my children – what would you like for Christmas?'

There was suddenly a lot of activity, shifting and sniffing and throat-clearing and eye-rolling and brow-furrowing. Mrs Grubson stirred the fire back into life and said, 'Best to go in age order children. Think carefully, tell your father and then be quiet,' she instructed.

She waited whilst everyone finally settled down and sat still. Grubson remained slightly slumped in his chair, Henri sitting bolt upright on his lap.

'Down Henri!' barked his mother. 'Get down from your father's lap – it'll only set off your wheezing again, sniffing in all that seaweed smell from your father's fur!'

Henri got down immediately, trotted to his stool at the table, jumped up and sat very still – taking extremely tiny breaths so as not to set off his wheezing – which would annoy his mother.

Chapter Two

What We Want For Christmas

Turning to face his eldest daughter, Grubson asked, 'Clementina, what would you like for Christmas?'

'Oh Papa,' simpered Clementina, 'you know how I long to be a concert pianist?' Grubson knew this well. 'You know how it is my destiny to be a world-famous concert pianist, playing in all the great music halls around the world?' Grubson heard about it every day. 'You know how I practise and practise until I have sore paws? ' This Grubson did not know. He wasn't sure this was entirely true. 'But still, I am never chosen to play at recitals. I could be a brilliant pianist, but what chance do I have if I only have this silly old piano inherited from your grandmother? If I had my own piano – my own *grand* piano, I would be a great pianist!' concluded Clementina, giving her father a winning smile.

Grubson nodded his head.

He looked at his eldest daughter very carefully and stared into her big brown eyes. He had brought his grandmother's piano all the way from Paris, but still Clementina had not played in any music recitals. Grubson had thought she was too lazy to practise and always took the easy option, blaming the piano because she wouldn't try hard enough with her scales and arpeggios and music-reading. But looking at Clementina now, Grubson wondered if he had let his daughter down.

'Let me see what I can do,' said Grubson quietly.

Pouring himself a tumbler of rum, Grubson asked his eldest son, 'Fabrice my boy, what would you like for Christmas?'

'A proper, professional, twenty-one-gear racing bike!' answered Fabrice immediately. 'I know I already have a bicycle, but it's rubbish and I just never win any races on it. And it gives me blisters in very inconvenient places. Training and practising sprint finishes is too much bother. I always finish last in races and I just want to get on a fantastic bike and win!'

Fabrice was quite worked up. He popped a sweetie in his mouth and chewed on it noisily, staring at his father.

Grubson swallowed his rum and nodded his head.

Fabrice's big brown eyes were locked onto him, pulling at his heart. Grubson had suspected that Fabrice was too lazy to train and too interested in food to be a good cyclist – his tubby frame had never looked quite right perched on top of a racing bike! He never stopped eating! Fabrice could be relied upon to have seconds at every meal and if there was more, he'd have thirds – AND lick his bowl clean. (And everyone else's bowl too if Mrs Grubson had allowed it.) Between meals he always had his nose in the pantry, sniffing out a little snack – biscuits, cakes, sweets, chocolates and crisps. But Grubson wanted Fabrice to be happy and decided to give this more thought.

'Thank you Fabrice, leave that with me,' he said, shifting to a more comfortable position.

His youngest daughter was desperate for her turn. Grubson asked, 'Bella my dear, what would you like for Christmas?'

Grubson's youngest daughter fluttered her eyelashes and peered up at her father, smiled sweetly and said, 'Well Papa, you know how pretty I am?' Grubson said nothing but continued to watch her with a kind expression on his face. 'Well, I know that you do know how pretty I am, because everyone in St Benfro probably tells you that! But the thing is that I could be even prettier! I know it's hard to imagine, because it must seem impossible that anyone could get any prettier than this, but I know I could be not only the prettiest girl in St Benfro, but quite likely the beautifullest girl in the whole country – in the whole wide world!'

'I see,' said Grubson, draining his glass.

'But people never do manage to see how pretty I am because they don't notice me. They always see Marianna Toppingham or Felicity Harvey-Witterington and not me because they always have the best dresses. They always have silk and satin and lacy bits and bows and if I had silk and satin and lacy bits and bows, I'd be noticed and have lots of friends! It's just not fair!'

Bella finally stopped. She was so angry that her voice had become high and yappy – the more she went on, the more she screeched. Her brow had become deeply furrowed again, her ears flattening back against her head, her eyes had disappeared behind her scrunched up cheeks and her bottom lip stuck out, revealing her pointy fang teeth. Not pretty.

Grubson nodded and cleared his throat.

He looked at his youngest daughter very carefully and tried to stare into her big brown eyes, which he knew were there somewhere, behind the scrunched up cheek fur. He had often thought that if she stopped constantly talking about herself and forcing people to pay attention to her, she could be very nice. But she was so angry so much of the time – screwing up her face and becoming really very ugly. She had dozens of party dresses but now it seemed none of them was good enough.

'I understand,' said Grubson quietly, 'I will give that some thought.'

Feeling terribly, terribly tired, Grubson looked in Henri's direction at the other end of the table.

'Henri, what would you like for Christmas?' asked Grubson.

From his stool, Henri could only just see over the table top if he lifted his chin up. Grubson watched as his youngest child nervously licked his lips and then ask his mother if he could be allowed to stand so he could see everyone. (This sort of behaviour was strictly forbidden at the table at meal-times.) Having gained Mrs Grubson's permission, Henri stood with his back legs on the stool and his front paws on the edge of the table. He beamed round at all the faces.

'What is it then Henri? What would you like for Christmas?' repeated Grubson.

'Well now . . .' puzzled Henri, 'that's a big question isn't it Papa?' Henri stared down at his paws. 'It's just that everyone else has asked for such big and impressive Christmas presents and I'm embarrassed to say . . .' he hesitated. 'I'm ashamed to say that my thing what . . . the thing that what . . . the thing what I was going to ask about for a Christmas pressie . . .' he was getting tongue-tied now, 'isn't nearly as big. Good. Nearly as big or good – so I feel silly to say it.'

'Oh for goodness sake Henri – spit it out!' snapped Clementina unkindly.

'I'm sorry,' said Henri, 'it's just that when Papa was describing Christmas it sounded wonderful. It sounded like everyone would be smiling and happy. . .' his voice trailed away, afraid of being sneered at by his older brother and sisters. 'And Papa has already said the thing that I most want for Christmas. So he will already be doing my Christmas present!'

'What DO you mean Henri?' asked Mrs Grubson. 'Now stop babbling and talking in riddles and explain yourself!'

'I want Papa to be home for Christmas! He has never managed to be home for Christmas before and my favourite thing is to sit on his knee, close to the fire and to feel the salt from the sea in his fur and to sniff the seaweed on his clothes and to listen to his stories of where he's been and to look at the charts and maps – so I can imagine. That's what I want for Christmas. Please. Thank you.' Henri removed his front paws from the table, replaced his bottom on the stool and there he sat – his ears just showing.

'Please Papa,' Henri's voice could just be heard.

Grubson gulped and nodded his head.

He looked down the table towards his youngest son and gazed fondly at the top of Henri's head. Of all his children who might have had reason to feel hard done by, or desperate to be noticed, or greedy for recognition or feel ugly and overlooked and angry, it might have been Henri.

Despite wheezing in the summer due to pollen and wheezing in the winter due to germs, Henri never complained. He always asked to join in bicycle rides and piano-playing and choosing dresses, but he was never allowed. He was always left alone in a quiet part of the house where his wheezing wouldn't annoy anyone. And all he wanted for Christmas was to be a happy family, all together and to have Grubson home from the sea.

'Thank you Henri,' Grubson said quietly. 'Let me see what I can do.'

After a short silence, Mrs Grubson stood up and addressed her assembled family, 'Well, that was certainly very interesting. Everyone has explained what they want for Christmas in great detail and, apart from Henri who didn't seem to understand the question and doesn't yet understand Christmas, everyone has been very clear. Time for bed children!'

Clementina, Fabrice, Bella and Henri all kissed Grubson and their mother good night and went to bed.

'Looks like you've got your work cut out Grubson,' said Mrs Grubson. 'Good night.'

And with that, she went to bed.

Grubson Pug's Christmas Voyage

Chapter Three

Christmas Shopping

The next morning, Grubson woke early.

He hadn't slept well; he'd had tormented dreams that he was Father Christmas and had to travel the seven seas and go shopping in every corner of the universe in order to provide presents for every single boy and girl in the world.

In his dream, Mrs Grubson was Mrs Christmas. But she wasn't kind and smiley; she wasn't helping Grubson to load his sleigh. She was mean and nagging and constantly looking at her watch to tell him that he was running out of time and still hadn't got enough presents.

The only helpful person in Grubson's nightmare had been a lovely little elf – called Henri.

Grubson had made up his mind – he wanted to make this the best Christmas for all his family. He crawled quietly out of bed and tip-toed all the way up to the attic and creaked open the door. Blinking into the dusty grey light, Grubson could just see the old sea chest which his father had passed on to him. Inside there was money, gold bars, jewellery and a bag of pearls. Some say there had been pirates in the family, but Grubson had never liked to ask too many questions about where this money and treasure had come from. However, it was his now and he had been saving it – keeping it secret from everyone. He knew that one day, this treasure might be needed: when he was too old to sail or if something happened to him whilst he was away at sea. This money was for emergencies only.

Well, Grubson felt that this Christmas was an emergency.

He dipped his paws into the treasure chest and pulled out fistfuls of money, some of the jewellery and put several of the pearls into a small drawstring bag. He stuffed all of this into his duffle bag and crept downstairs and out of the house before anyone else was awake.

Grubson boarded The Beagle and told his surprised crew that they had one more voyage to make before Christmas.

This is where you need a few introductions to the crew!

Lefty Gibbet:
Lefty didn't like the word "mongrel"; it gave people the wrong idea. He preferred to call himself a "sea gypsy". His mother was a Lurcher, the daughter of a game-keeper and his father, a Greyhound, had been a fire-eater with a circus. Lefty's father had gone to Italy on a short tour for the Venice Festival and had never bothered to come back. Lefty's mother had been heart-broken, but her best friends said they'd never trusted him and she was probably better off without him.

Mostly black-furred, Lefty had a wiry ginger goatee beard and ginger wisps in his eyebrows and ear fur – one of which was pierced. He was tall and strong and had several tattoos – the largest of which was a heart and anchor. He had this tattoo done for the only girl he had ever truly loved: a pert little Poodle from Paris called Mimi. He had loved her enough to stay home from sea and get a job in the market, in the hope of marrying her.

But Mimi had other ideas. She disappeared one night, tip-toeing out of the house whilst Lefty was asleep. When he woke in the morning, there was no Mimi. Only a photograph of herself and on the back she had written one word: "sorry". He heard later that she moved to Monte Carlo to work in the casinos, but he had never seen her again.

After Mimi left, he decided to go back to sea where he felt he belonged. He had joined the crew of The Beagle and Grubson was pleased to have him aboard because he was reliable, frightened of nothing and a very good sailor.

Lefty's main duty on board The Beagle was to make sure all the ropes and rigging were in full working order and he knew thirty-seven different kinds of knots! (He always used to joke that he could tie every kind of knot except the one with Mimi.)

As part of the crew, Lefty was probably the quietest. He didn't like sitting around on deck gossiping and making small talk. But he loved a good argument! Arguing and sailing were when Lefty felt most alive.

Sebastian Barafundle:

Sebastian Barafundle on the other hand was a well-bred Spaniel who had run away to sea to escape his grandmother, Lady Barafundle! She was planning to marry him off to Cecilia Savilton – the daughter of a wealthy hotel owner. Sebastian and Cecilia did not get on. They never had. Even as pups they used to fight and squabble over every last squeaky toy and morsel of food. As they got older Sebastian couldn't stand the squabbling and he used to let Cecilia do whatever she wanted, just to avoid an argument. She really took advantage of this and pushed him about and ordered him around and laughed at him for being so feeble.

He never used to laugh at her although he would have had a very good excuse! She had a lisp which meant she couldn't pronounce her "Ss". She couldn't even say her own name *without sounding very silly or spraying anyone who happened to be near her!*

The Barafundle family was a very pure pedigree – they had royalty and prime ministers in their background. Lady Barafundle's father had been a gambler and had lost a lot of the family's money in dice games and poker matches which went on for days. First he lost his own money then he borrowed money from family and friends and lost that too. The only way he could pay back the money he had borrowed was by selling farms and land and even a castle which had been in the family for hundreds of years.

This meant that Lady Barafundle was posh but very short of money and she wanted Sebastian to marry Cecilia because she was rich.

Mr Savilton wanted Cecilia to marry Sebastian because he had good breeding – and the Savilton family didn't have any of that!

On the morning that Sebastian ran, Mrs Grubson had been in town with her eldest son Fabrice, who was a very small puppy at that time. Fabrice had just learned to ride his first tricycle and was wobbling his way down the cobbled streets of St Benfro. He had stopped in the middle of the street to get off and look at the saddle (which was already giving him blisters) when Sebastian ran round the corner at full pelt. He saw the tricycle, but, too late to stop or avoid it, he skidded towards it, caught his legs on the handlebars and ended up riding it – shooting all the way down the steep hill at top speed!

He couldn't stop when he got to the harbour wall and the front wheel hit a kerb stone and pitched Sebastian way up into the air, over the handlebars and into the sea! Grubson and Lefty had seen all this from the deck of The Beagle and they hauled the very shocked and very soaked Sebastian out of the water and on board the ship. And that is how Sebastian ran away to sea.

Since then, Lefty and Sebastian had travelled many hundreds of miles around the world with Grubson. They were a trusty crew and the best of friends. They occasionally fell out of course and then there would be a big argument or a big silence and no one would speak for a couple of days. None of them enjoyed the days of silence and only Lefty enjoyed the arguing.

What happened to Cecilia you may ask? Cecilia married Thackeray Sissingthistle, Duke of Straithness. This means two things. Firstly, it is now safe for Sebastian to return home because he can't be married off to the awful Cecilia. Secondly, it means that she has a very silly name which she can't pronounce and that serves her right!

Duchess Cecilia Savilton-Sissingthistle of Straithness!

Back to the story!

The early morning sea fog was still hanging over the bay as Grubson boarded The Beagle. Lefty and Sebastian were surprised to see him as no voyage had been planned until after Christmas. They were delighted; they got so bored just sitting around in the harbour.

Having stowed his treasure-filled duffle bag underneath his hammock, Grubson unfurled his sea chart and went on deck for a chat with Lefty and Sebastian. And Marjorie.

Not strictly a crew member, Marjorie went everywhere The Beagle went. She was officially Grubson's parrot and when needed, she would sit on his shoulder and shriek threats at vagabonds and customs inspectors. Marjorie had come with the ship when Grubson bought The Beagle. She was a descendent of the original owner's parrot and very proud of that fact.

Grubson and Marjorie were very clear about where they stood with one another: he did not own her. She could come and go as she pleased, as a free spirit, but as long as she chose to stay aboard The Beagle, Grubson as captain would have the last word on all sailing decisions.

So, Grubson sat down for a chat with Lefty, Sebastian and Marjorie. And Banzai.

Perhaps I should have mentioned Banzai before – you need to know about him too!

Banzai:

Banzai was the ship's cat. He was a Siamese and had silky white fur and a grey nose, ears and legs. And blue eyes. He was really rather beautiful and looked very refined but he didn't behave that way! He wore a bandana around his head, constantly chewed garlic and when he wasn't busy on board ship, he'd be practising judo or kickboxing or doing press-ups to stay strong.

Ten years before, when Grubson had bought The Beagle, it came with a parrot, but no ship's cat. Every ship needs a cat and Grubson didn't want to set sail without one, so he searched the back streets of St Benfro for a likely cat.

He knew Banzai was the one for him when he went into The Three Buccaneers for a drink and noticed a crowd of sailors gathered around a table in an alcove.

Banzai was arm-wrestling any sea-dog who fancied his chances against a weedy cat! A carpet bag was wedged underneath his stool, attached to one of his legs by a chain.

Banzai had a foolproof plan – it worked every time! He would wander into a port town where no one knew him and sit meekly in the corner of the baddest bar in town and watch the sailors coming in and staggering out. He would soon be noticed, being the only cat in the bar and as soon as he was noticed, he would do what cats do better than anyone else in the world. He would stare at a sailor.

Just stare – his blue eyes shining out of his gloomy corner.

And the sailors did not like that. It made the fur on their backs stand on end and make them look scared – or angry. So rather than look scared, they'd get angry.

'Oi cat – whatchya think yer starin' at?'

Banzai would then yawn – a really massive cat yawn – which made his ears go flat down on his head and made the whites of his eyes show as he revealed a mouthful of shiny sharp teeth and a barbed tongue.

Ending his yawn and licking his lips he would proceed to pick a bit of fish from between his teeth and say, 'I'm looking at ... nothing ... nothing but a scaredy doggy.'

This would make the sailor furious and he'd immediately challenge Banzai to a fight.

'Righty,' Banzai would say, 'I like fighting! Pistols? Boxing? Or swords? Anything you like except arm-wrestling. I'm only a little scrawny cat and I don't like arm-wrestling – but the choice is yours. Doggy.'

And the silly sailor would always say, 'Arm-wrestling!'

And that was Banzai's favourite sport. Sailor after sailor would challenge Banzai to an arm-wrestling contest in the corner of the pub and a lot of money changed hands. Banzai always won.

Grubson had never really liked cats because all the ones he'd ever met were either vain and soppy, or arrogant and terribly snooty. But Banzai was different: he was exciting and rather naughty.

When Grubson saw him in The Three Buccaneers, he offered Banzai the chance to sail with The Beagle. As it turned out, Banzai had been looking for a way to get out of town for a while because he was beginning to get a bad name. He jumped at the chance to join the ship and sail to lots of different towns where no one knew him and he could continue to arm-wrestle silly sailors.

Back to the story!

Grubson sat down for a chat with Lefty, Sebastian, Marjorie and Banzai.

He explained how they had some fast sailing ahead of them and many ports to visit. His Christmas shopping voyage was as follows:

St Benfro to Seville in Spain – to find beautiful dresses for Bella.

Seville to St Malo in France – to find a racing bike for Fabrice.

St Malo to London in England – to find a grand piano for Clementina.

London to St Benfro – by Christmas Eve for Henri.

This was a tall order! So many places and so little time!

Lefty sucked in his breath between his teeth. Sebastian nervously smoothed the glossy fur on his ears. Marjorie tutted loudly. Banzai whistled a long low note and looked doubtful. And Grubson ignored them all, went on deck, untied the ropes holding his ship in her mooring and took his position at the helm of The Beagle.

Christmas Shopping

Grubson Pug's Christmas Voyage

Chapter Four

Seville

By the eleventh of December, The Beagle was safely moored in the harbour of Seville.

Even on a cold, crisp December morning, the sun shone brightly and the majestic buildings of Seville were a warm honey colour. The narrow streets spiralled up from the harbour and widened out into big squares full of orange trees and fountains.

Lefty and Sebastian got busy swabbing the decks, checking the sails and buying food and water ready for the next part of the voyage. Marjorie was sitting in the wheelhouse, dozing in the winter sunshine. Banzai heaved his carpet bag onto his shoulder and went looking for a bar in a backstreet; he was thrilled at the thought of a new place where no one knew him and the chance to arm-wrestle a lot of unsuspecting Spanish sailors!

Grubson set off into town to find a dress-maker. It didn't take him long. He followed his nose from the harbour and made a few enquiries along the way. Before long he was standing outside Senor Castanet's impressive shop in the city's most expensive street.

Despite the sunshine, Grubson shivered in the sea wind which had followed him up from the harbour. He pulled his old coat tightly around him as he peered at the winter fashions in the window. Thinking about Bella, Grubson tried to imagine her wearing the red velvets, white furs and emerald green satins. Suddenly Grubson found himself dreaming into a very gruff face – the frowning and irritated face of a heavily built Labrador wearing a maroon uniform with gold braid on the shoulders; his brass buttons were shining, his boots were gleaming – his face was sneering.

Grubson realised he must look a very sorry sight, staring in at the window. His old coat was stretched around him and fraying at the edges; sea salt had matted his fur and he thought his nose might be dripping a bit. I must look like an old tramp, he thought.

He wasn't going to be put off by a snooty old Labrador; he was on a mission to get Bella's dresses and he had no time to waste, so he straightened his back and approached the shop door.

The Labrador was there before him, blocking the doorway and staring up into the air. Grubson nodded to him and said, 'Ola! Hello! I have come to buy a beautiful collection of dresses from Senor Castanet.'

The Labrador lifted an eyebrow in a very disbelieving way:

'I don't-a think so, senor. We 'ave no clothes which could possibly be right for you. I am so sorry but I must ask-a you to leave. To go. Hasta la vista, senor!'

Grubson was impatient now and anxious to buy Bella's present and get back to The Beagle.

'You don't understand,' stumbled Grubson, 'I must see Senor Castanet . . .' He squeezed past the Labrador and into the warmth of the shop.

'Oh I understand very well senor!' shouted the Labrador. 'You come in 'ere with your steeeenking coat and your not-very-nice boots – to get warm! You steenk out our beautiful shop with the steenk of the seaweed – to get warm! Now understand THIS senor – you must GO!'

Just as the doorman was about to kick Grubson out,

a tiny Chihuahua wearing very tight black velvet flares and long lacy cuffs appeared from the back of the shop. Senor Castanet!

'Julius!' screamed Senor Castanet. 'What on-a earth ees going on 'ere? Eh? I go out back for a few minutes and come in to find you growling at my customers!'

Julius explained how a smelly tramp had tried to come in and he was spoiling the look of Senor Castanet's shop.

The minuscule Armando Castanet stood, hands on hips like a pair of scissors, listening. When Julius had finished, Armando said nothing but inclined his head towards Grubson, big ears fluffed out and ready to hear his side of the story. He listened, unblinking, as Grubson explained that he realised he looked like a tramp but he had travelled a very long way on his ship and had walked in the cold wind through the city to come and buy beautiful dresses for his daughter Bella.

'I am very upset by this welcome,' concluded Grubson, wheezing as he unbuttoned his coat to reach inside and pull out his dog-eared wallet which was bulging with money.

'And so am I!' squealed Armando Castanet. He rushed across the marble floor, jumped onto a display shelf full of perfumes and growled at Julius.

'Ow many times Julius?' enquired the Chihuahua.
'Ow many times does I have to keep-a telling to you?' he
drew in a deep breath, 'NEVER to be judging a book by
the cover!'

Stretching a perfectly manicured paw out in Grubson's
direction, he continued to Julius, 'E may look like a tramp!
'E may SMELL like a tramp! But 'e EESN'T a tramp!'

'Si senor,' whispered Julius, head hanging down.

Armando jumped down from the display stand and,
as if none of that had happened, turned graciously to

Grubson and said, 'Good afternoon senor. Welcome to my shop. 'Ow may I 'elp you?'

Grubson told him about Bella and her love of beautiful dresses. He showed Senor Castanet photographs of Bella at various parties and beauty contests, twirling and showing off and scowling.

Senor Castanet listened very quietly and when Grubson had finished, he nodded, picked a speck of something invisible from his jacket, stood up and said, 'I 'ave plenty dresses which would be perfect for young Bella. Fantastic colours of satins, silks and lacy bits and bows, suitable for all parties and competitions.'

Grubson was relieved to hear this; it had been quite a struggle to get into this shop after all and he was hopeful that Senor Castanet would be able to supply exactly what Bella wanted.

Armando squeezed Grubson's knee in a reassuring way, and sat him down in a velvet antique chair before skipping the length of the marble-floored shop and whisking behind a billowing satin curtain – out of sight.

Julius appeared with a tray of coffee and hand-made biscuits.

'For you senor,' said Julius, forcing a smile across his lips. 'Please, you must tell me if there is anything else you need.'

And before leaving Grubson to enjoy his drink and treats, he quickly snatched a bottle of perfume from the display stand, squeaked out, 'Permit me senor' and doused Grubson in the citrus scents of "Armando No.1".

Julius was gone.

Left alone, Grubson sniffed the air and sniffed his fur. He had to admit that as long as the perfume didn't set off his wheezing, he rather liked smelling sweetly of lemons and grapefruit. It made a change from seaweed and mackerel. He smiled to himself as he tucked into his coffee and biscuits, smelling very expensive.

A few moments later, Senor Castanet stepped dramatically from behind the satin curtains and smoothed down the already-smooth fur on his head before announcing, 'And-a now senor, please to permit my bee-yootiful models as they parade up and-a down to demonstrate what I 'ave chosen for la Bella's wardrobe.'

With that, a line of very thin, very smiley girls – Whippets, Poodles and Chihuahuas, stalked out from behind the curtain, one by one. They marched and twirled and paraded the dresses for Grubson to see. They were enchanting: jewel coloured satins with lace necklines and big bows on the back; pale pink silk, wafting in pleats and folds of taffeta; fur-trimmed gowns which splayed onto the floor. Grubson was spellbound – he sat transfixed, a biscuit halfway to his mouth.

When Grubson had seen twenty-five of the finest dresses and ball gowns Seville had to offer, he had a decision to make: he couldn't take all the dresses, but he wanted to take six. How could he choose which ones would make Bella look most pretty? He asked Armando for advice.

The Chihuahua put his hands on his hips and looked up to the ceiling, 'The theeng is senor,' said Senor Castanet seriously, 'there is-a something what I very much want you to understand. Eet is true – I am very creative and make the most fantastic dresses in Seville – in Spain! They are beautiful shapes and colours and I use only the finest materials. They will make any girl look glamorous. But in order for her to look pretty and BE beautiful, she must be kind and generous and funny and she must SMILE!'

Armando began to strut up and down in front of Grubson to demonstrate his words.

'Theese is no good if she is to be a big show off!' he pulled a snooty face and put his nose in the air.

'No good if she is to stump up and down, wagging 'er behind and with 'er 'ead 'anging down.' More demonstration. 'No good if she is to be looking at 'er friends with jealous eyes and an angry heart! It is no good for 'er to frown and make lines in 'er face and show 'er fangs!'

Grubson was quiet.

'Do you understand senor?' asked Armando. 'Do you think you can 'elp for Bella to understand?' Grubson could clearly picture Bella's angry grimace as soon as anyone tried to point out any of her faults but he would find a way to make Bella listen to Senor Castanet's wise words if she was ever to be pretty and popular.

Sometime later, Grubson left Senor Castanet's shop, waved off by Armando and Julius. He had six bags, each one containing a fabulous dress for Bella.

Chapter Five

St Malo

The voyage from Seville to St Malo took The Beagle up the Portuguese coast and through the Bay of Biscay – which was pretty choppy. Lefty and Sebastian had loaded a cargo of oranges on board whilst they were in Seville, knowing that they would be able to sell these back in St Benfro – perfect to put in the toes of Christmas stockings! Apart from these oranges and the dresses for Bella, The Beagle carried no other cargo so that she could sail as fast as possible.

The days were passing quickly and by the time Grubson

and his crew arrived in St Malo, it was the seventeenth of December. It was late afternoon when they moored The Beagle. The crew were very tired and Grubson left them to sleep whilst he went into town in search of the famous bicycle shop – owned by a Monsieur Frank Aquitaine, a Whippet from Gascony.

Grubson walked briskly along the sea wall to the huge medieval buttresses which encircled the oldest parts of St Malo. Within the town walls, Grubson found the narrow streets bustling with shoppers, street performers, artists, children and dogs. He made a few enquiries and soon found the shop he was looking for.

A bell jingled as Grubson pushed opened the door and stepped down into the cave-like shop. It was packed with bicycles – they were standing in rows, ranked far back into the depths of the narrow shop which extended much further than you would think when standing outside.

Grubson looked around for any sign of life and called, 'Bonjour? Hello? Hell-oo?'

Behind him, he heard a very loud sniffing sound. Grubson turned around to see the refined and intelligent face of a Whippet – slightly greying around the temples, just tucking a handkerchief into the cuff of his very large jumper.

Monsieur Aquitaine lifted an enquiring ear and said,

'Pardon monsieur. I am very sorry – I 'ave a most 'orrible cold! Welcome to my shop monsieur. 'Ow may I 'elp you?'

Grubson explained about Fabrice's love of cycling and how he wanted the best racing bike money could buy so that he would not get blisters in awkward places and could then win races. Monsieur Aquitaine listened intently – nodding and sniffing and wiping his nose.

'Allow me to show you some of my most fastest and lightest bicycles. These are fantastique!'

Monsieur Aquitaine enthusiastically showed Grubson his vast and varied race-winning collection of bicycles. As he talked, he trailed a paw lovingly around the curling handlebars, stroked and squeezed the narrow tyres and rippled his claws around the shining silver spokes. Having examined at least thirty bicycles – each one as lean and built for speed as Frank Aquitaine himself, Grubson was pretty confused. He didn't know which one to choose and asked for advice.

Monsieur Aquitaine blew his nose and, unwrapping a throat sweet, beckoned to Grubson to follow him to the back of the shop, down a spiral staircase and into the basement below.

It was huge! The tiny shop front gave no hint of how far back the space inside extended and how could anyone

guess that in the basement, the shop burrowed away and doubled back underneath the road! Of course, there were many more bicycles down here too, but the biggest surprise of all was the trophies!

Cabinets, shelves, cupboards, display stands and upturned crates were full of glittering shields and cups and medals. The walls were covered in photographs of Frank Aquitaine being awarded prizes for cycle races – standing small and proud in his lycra cycling shorts and brightly coloured tops, spraying champagne from his winner's pedestal all over a cheering crowd!

Grubson was open-mouthed – unable to speak.

The Whippet popped the throat sweet into his mouth and immediately started to suck loudly as the treacly syrup soothed his throat.

'Please . . . (slurp) . . . (suck, slurp) . . . please . . . call me . . . (slurp, suck, slurp) . . . Frank. (slurp, slurp) . . . It is quite a sight eh? I am . . . (sucketty slurp) . . . 'ow you say, very proud.'

Grubson found his voice at last and still gawping, he asked which bicycle had won him the most of these trophies.

(Slurp . . . slurp . . . suck . . . sschlepp . . . schlurp . . .)

Frank gained control of his throat sweet and looked Grubson in the eye. 'You must understand somesing 'ere

Grubson. And Fabrice must understand this too. Sure, the bicycle you ride is very important, but these trophies are not won by the bicycle! No! These trophies are won by the rider! By the rider who gives his life to racing – the rider who eats, sleeps, dreams and breathes to race and to WIN!' He paused to do a bit more slurping and blow his nose. 'The trophy goes to the rider who trains every day, in sun, snow and rain. The rider who cycles up the steepest mountains and builds 'is strength is the rider who will win. Without these things, Fabrice will never win – not even on the best bicycle in the world.'

Grubson had known this in his heart and he pictured Fabrice's rotund body squeezed into his cycling shorts, wobbling about on his bicycle, complaining about blisters. He would need to put Fabrice on a diet straight away and help him get into training. This wasn't going to be easy, but it would be the only way to help Fabrice win races.

Grubson left Frank's shop with a sparkling new racing bike. He proudly wheeled it through the streets of St Malo, looking in through shop windows at the brightly lit Christmas displays as he went. It would soon be Christmas and he still had one more present to get before he could head home.

St Malo

Chapter Six

London

The Beagle hurried across the Channel in double quick time, a sharp Easterly wind filling her sails and blowing her back towards London. On the twentieth of December, Grubson steered his ship past the Channel Islands and with help from Lefty and Sebastian, he guided her to the mouth of the River Thames.

There were warnings that the weather would soon change, bringing gales and rain from the west during the next day or so and that would make sailing very difficult. Banzai went into the hold to make sure the cargo was secure.

He added extra ropes to the bicycle and crates of oranges which were lashed to the side timbers. Bella's dresses swung from a central beam and he hammered nails through their hangers so that they could not possibly fall down. He took the lid off a massive woven hamper which he and Marjorie had bought in St Malo – it smelled delicious – to him. Full of garlic and very ripe cheeses, the odour rushed from the basket, filled the hold and almost knocked him out! But Banzai was made of stern stuff and having had a little nibble of garlic (his favourite treat) he wrapped a long strap of leather around the hamper and pulled it tightly shut with a hook. He smiled to himself as he thought of Christmas Day – lying in his hammock, scoffing cheese and garlic!

He checked to make sure his carpet bag was safely stowed in his secret cubby hole and rejoined the rest of the crew, taking his place at the top of the mast, up in the crow's nest.

Late that afternoon, The Beagle sailed carefully up the Thames, past the Royal Observatory, round the Isle of Dogs, underneath Tower Bridge and found a good spot to moor. Tired but excited, Grubson and his crew got busy; they rushed to the brightly lit shops to finish their Christmas shopping before it would be time to hurry back home to St Benfro by Christmas Eve. All apart from Banzai – who picked up his carpet bag and went into town looking for sailors to arm-wrestle.

Grubson's grandmother had once told him about a very special piano shop in Elephant and Castle (where there wasn't actually an elephant or a castle, but Grubson presumed there must have been once). He got his map of London and found his way there as quickly as he could, feeling the wind begin to turn colder and he could smell snow in the air.

The piano shop was owned by a Dachshund called Fraulein Schneerer. She had a German father and a French mother and lived in England – she considered herself truly continental and very sophisticated! Grubson was cold as he stomped through the wind and rain in the failing light. He ran into the warm shop from the freezing pavement outside.

Inside was another world! The shop was vast and airy – a central staircase swept up three storeys to a glass domed roof and the huge space twinkled and glimmered with hundreds of candles and tiny lights sparkling in every corner. Fraulein Schneerer's shop was filled with pianos of every description: uprights, grand pianos, baby grands, harpsichords and even an antique piano which had once belonged to Queen Victoria. The highly polished instruments were gleaming and reflecting the light from the myriad of tiny bright candles and crystal chandeliers.

Grubson thought he could hear music being played from somewhere high up above him – the treble notes chirping like birds around the domed roof and the bass notes thundering around his feet like a herd of buffalo. There was no sign of Fraulein Schneerer.

'Guten tag! Hello?' called Grubson. The music stopped. Still no sign of Fraulein Schneerer, but Grubson could distinctly smell the sweet slightly sickly scent of mimosa – a favourite with older ladies.

From above, a husky, whispery voice said, 'Guten tag. I hope zat you enjoyed my music? Velcome to my shop and how may I help you?'

Grubson peered up to the top of the staircase and saw the delicate and inquisitive face of Fraulein Schneerer – she removed her half-moon spectacles to reveal the long lashes which shaded her dark eyes and ran a paw through her silky ear-fur.

Grubson had just taken a deep breath and braced himself to begin the long climb up the staircase to join her, when suddenly she appeared at his side! Slightly shocked and a tiny bit frightened at the speed with which she had descended the staircase, Grubson stammered slightly as he began to explain about Clementina and her dream to become a concert pianist.

Fraulein Schneerer listened very politely and when Grubson had finished speaking, she replaced her glasses on the tip of her long and very refined nose. 'Allow me to show you some of my most perfectly tuned and beautifully made grand pianos. They are truly wunderbar!'

Gliding from one instrument to the next, Fraulein Schneerer proudly demonstrated the sounds of her pianos with enthusiasm. Her paws whisked up and down the keys, trickling tiny little feathery notes out of the trebles and booming big bass sounds with gusto. Grubson was enchanted by the music and by the pianos themselves – each huge lid was lifted onto a prop and revealed the harp-like arrangement of strings and tiny wooden hammers beneath. These pianos were grand indeed and Grubson could easily imagine Clementina playing at recitals.

Grubson was not at all musical himself and had inherited none of his grandmother's talent. Which piano would be best for Clementina? He asked Fraulein Schneerer to help him decide.

'I hope you do not zink for one minute zat to buy Clementina a grand piano would enable her to become an overnight piano genius! In order to do zis, she must spend many hours, every day – EVERY DAY – for many years in ze practising of her SCALES up and down and ze ARPEGGIOS up and down and ze READING of music and ze UNDERSTANDING of rhythm and ze FEELING OF LOVE for music, music, MUSIC! Only when all zis is done can Clementina begin to become a musician. It is very important that you and Clementina understand how much work it takes to play ze piano WELL!'

When she had finished speaking, Fraulein Schneerer took a tiny mirror from her handbag and applied some red lipstick and a drop more mimosa perfume. This gave Grubson time to think about what she had said.

He had secretly known for years that Clementina's terrible piano playing was nothing to do with her claws catching on the old piano keys. It was nothing to do with the age of the piano. It was it was everything to do with the fact that she never practised. If she couldn't play a piece of music straight away, she lost patience, blamed her claws or blamed the piano and stomped out of the room.

He decided that when he went home, he would sit down with Clementina and explain Fraulein Schneerer's words and find her the best piano teacher in St Benfro. Grubson left the glittering piano shop having ordered a grand piano and hurried back across London to The Beagle and her crew.

Early the next morning, a huge crate containing the grand piano packed in calico and sawdust was delivered to the ship and lowered into the hold. It just squeezed through the biggest hatch door and Banzai set about bolting it to the floor.

Chapter Seven

Shipshape

It was the twenty-first of December and Grubson, Lefty, Sebastian, Marjorie and Banzai were sitting around the charts on board The Beagle. They were very quiet. It was a long way home and even here in the shelter of the high embankment, the December wind was ruffling and shaking the furled sails. Unseen fingers were pulling at the ropes, tightly lashed around the canvas – loosening the grip. A big storm was on the way from the Atlantic Ocean, making the homeward voyage difficult and much slower.

Grubson had drawn two lines on the chart. One line showed the safest way home. The other line showed the shortest way home.

Everyone was quiet. They were all tired and they all wanted to be home but each of them was worried by the forecast of heavy weather, high seas and strong winds.

Grubson made up his mind and Marjorie flapped away off his shoulder and onto her perch as he stood up and said, 'We sail in the morning – first tide. There is a chance that we can get home before the worst of the weather hits us and so we will take the shortest – fastest – way home.'

Everyone nodded silently; each of them knew that the shortest way home not only meant the fastest but the most dangerous way too. They left the chart room to start the important jobs they needed to do before setting sail the next day.

Grubson went below decks into the damp gloom of the hold and surveyed the cargo of Christmas presents he had travelled so far to gather.

The racing bike was shining brightly, gleaming in its dark corner where Banzai had tightly secured it to the timbers. Grubson fondly patted the saddle of the bike and moved on to Clementina's piano. Banzai had bolted the crate to the floor so that it wouldn't slip and slide across the hold in stormy seas. Nothing would move that. Helping himself to an orange, Grubson stacked the crates of fruit into another corner and tied a big net over them so that they wouldn't roll about.

Bella's dresses were suspended from a central beam and he admired the colours and careful stitching of all the lace and bows. He was pleased to see that they weren't hanging directly over the smelly crate of cheese and garlic which Marjorie and Banzai had bought in France. Grubson wheezed slightly as his nose filled with the strong wafts coming from a dark part of the hold where he hardly ever went.

Following his nose, Grubson went to see if the stinky crate was safely stowed. As he bent to look at it, he noticed Banzai's carpet bag in its secret cubby hole. So that's where he keeps it, thought Grubson, wondering what on earth Banzai actually kept in that bag – with its huge buckle.

Whilst in London, he had bought a present – a proper secret surprise Christmas present, for Mrs Grubson. He had bought her a small brooch in the shape of a ship in full sail – just like The Beagle. Made of gold and with a diamond at the top of the mast, it was very expensive and Grubson certainly didn't want to risk losing it if he was being thrown around the ship during a storm. Where could he safely put it?

Looking round the hold, Grubson's gaze fell once

more onto Banzai's mysterious carpet bag. The cat had never revealed to anyone what he kept in his big old bag, but it was obviously very precious to him. He never left The Beagle without it and when he was out in the dockside bars arm-wrestling with sailors, he always kept it under his stool, chained to his leg. Banzai guarded it with his life and Grubson could think of nowhere safer to keep the little golden brooch.

Having unbuckled the ornate metal clasp on top of the bag, Grubson quickly slipped in the brooch. He didn't waste time nosing about to see what Banzai kept in there – he couldn't risk being found with his paw – or his nose, inside someone else's bag. What would Banzai think? And he didn't want to upset that cat – he was harder and tougher than he looked! So Grubson quickly re-buckled the carpet bag and pushed it back into Banzai's little cubby hole.

Everything seemed to be safe and shipshape! Pleased with his work, Grubson went up on deck to see how preparations were getting on.

Lefty's talent was with all the ropes. Whilst Grubson had been checking the precious cargo, Lefty had been climbing the rigging to check that every rope and every knot was strong. Any signs of fraying meant replacing them – Lefty could not risk snapped ropes in the middle of a gale.

Sebastian had spent the afternoon unfurling, hoisting and checking every stitch in every sail. Where he found signs of seams coming apart, he fed strong thread through the eye of his huge sail-maker's needle and stitched the seams again. His paws were quite raw from pushing his needle through the thick canvas sailcloth.

Banzai had put his time to good use too – he had been up to the crow's nest at the top of the highest mast to make sure it was safe and he had spent a long time oiling his telescope, whistling to himself happily.

Banzai's telescope was a beautiful brass antique which he had won from another ship's cat in a bar in Valparaiso. This had been a particularly tough arm-wrestling contest – cat against cat – but Banzai had won.

The telescope was one of Banzai's favourite things – it was hand-made for a cat and was therefore just the right size to hold to his eye and just the right weight to hold steady. When it was extended, it was just the right length for a cat's arm and he could see clearly for many miles when he looked through it. And when it was not in use, it collapsed into itself, very small.

Then chewing away on a big bulb of garlic, he had swabbed the decks, muttering under his breath (his smelly breath) every time Grubson or Sebastian or Lefty walked across his beautiful clean and shiny boards in their knobbly old muddy boots. And finally he had gone below to check the hold and make sure there were no mice thinking of joining them for the voyage home.

Marjorie had had a lovely afternoon drinking tea and eating tiny sandwiches with her best friend Topper, a cockatoo who lived in Buckingham Palace! Topper and his owner were on the gardening staff at the palace and he had many interesting tales to tell about the royal corgis and the Queen (or "The Boss" as he called her).

So, with The Beagle all prepared for the final part of

her journey, Grubson and his crew and Marjorie went to bed early to get a good night's sleep. They would need their wits about them the next day. Swinging in their hammocks they went to sleep and dreamed of Christmas and dry land and garlic, which somehow got into everyone's noses as Banzai snored out great wafts of it.

Chapter Eight

Christmas Preparations

Meanwhile, back at home in St Benfro, there had been preparations too.

Henri had been helping his mother to make the Christmas pudding. Everyone came into the kitchen to stir the pudding mixture and make a Christmas wish. Although this had to be done secretly, Henri knew exactly what everyone wished for: Fabrice was wearing his cycling shorts, despite the cold weather, so it didn't take a genius to guess his wish. Clementina was humming piano concertos whilst she was doing her stirring and wishing, so Henri was in no doubt about that one. Bella was actually wearing her school uniform when she came into the kitchen, even though it was the Christmas holidays. She said this was because she had nothing pretty enough to wear for Christmas and rather than wear her ugly old dresses, she would wear her school uniform which was at least supposed to be horrid. No prizes for guessing her Christmas wish!

This just left Henri. Alone in the kitchen, the last to make his Christmas Pudding Wish, Henri stirred the sticky mixture as fast as he could. Balanced on tiptoe and heaving the wooden spoon round with both arms, he almost fell into the bowl in his efforts to make a really good wish. Then he squeezed his eyes shut and pictured Grubson on board The Beagle, sailing home in time for Christmas.

He thought his wish as loudly as he possibly could.

When the pudding mixture was baking in the oven and after he had washed up the bowls and spoons, when he had swept the floor free of egg shells, flour and sugar grains, Henri pulled on his sou'wester hat and coat and ran off in the direction of the harbour.

Sitting on the harbour wall, Henri strained to see through the driving rain. Monastery Island which was very nearby had almost entirely disappeared inside the heavy grey storm clouds. His big worried eyes were pinned on the horizon, searching for a huge white sail and The Beagle coming home.

There was nothing. Not a single fishing boat or ship to be seen; all the sailors had heard the forecast and made sure they were on dry land. A few seagulls were circling high above, keeping their distance from the crashing white crests of the waves. Henri could just hear them calling to one another, shrieking warnings about the storm out at sea.

Henri jumped up and down, trying to attract their attention, 'Have you seen The Beagle out at sea? Have you seen Captain Grubson and his ship when you were out there looking for fish? Can you tell me where my papa is?' But Henri's words were no sooner out of his mouth than they were whipped away by the wind and out of earshot.

Henri sat down and stared at the sea. It was a great big heaving grey cauldron of crashing waves. It roared and thrashed against the rocks and boomed against the harbour wall, like a huge angry animal.

The wind was howling back at the sea and Henri imagined he could hear all kinds of story-book giant dogs, growling and barking angrily. He was frightened. He didn't like to think of Grubson out there on The Beagle being thrown about on the swirling sea like an old slipper.

Henri set off again at a trot, along the harbour wall towards the tallest house in town – Gunfort Mansions. The home of his friend, Horatio Fox.

Grubson Pug's Christmas Voyage

Chapter Nine

The Storm

MEANWHILE, BACK ON BOARD THE
BEAGLE ...
Grubson was standing at the helm,
hanging onto the ship's wheel with all his strength. The
Beagle was being carried high up to the tops of towering
waves before crashing down the other side to bang into
the churning seawater, before the next wave thrashed
across the deck, throwing anything that wasn't tied down
overboard. It was almost impossible for Grubson to steer
and he struggled to make sure that they were staying on

course and not heading for rocks.

Squinting up through the stinging rain, Grubson could just make out the thin, wiry form of Banzai in the crow's nest, his eye to the telescope. He had tied himself to the mast and was shrieking great excited yelps and scowling at the waves as he took one drenching after another.

Grubson was shouting urgent instructions to Lefty and Sebastian. They swung from ropes as they hauled on the sails to let them out as large as they would go, or furled them in and tied them against the masts. The salty seawater stung their eyes until they could hardly see and they couldn't feel their feet as they waded about on deck, sloshing through the cold water. They were hungry and tired but there wasn't a minute to rest as they battled against the raging waves to help The Beagle find her way home through the storm.

Below decks, in the galley, Marjorie was swinging about frantically on her perch. Her small eyes were wide with fear as she ducked the pots and pans, knives, dishes and bottles which were flying around. Her clawed feet were white with the effort of hanging on and her little black tongue whipped in and out of her beak as she squawked prayers to every saint she could think of to save The Beagle and her crew.

Below Marjorie, down in the hold, the bike, the

oranges, the dresses, the cheese and garlic hamper, the piano and the carpet bag held firm. Safe and dry.

Grubson who had thought he couldn't be any more frightened, suddenly felt his knees go to jelly as he heard Banzai scream! He looked up to see his cat untie himself from the mast in twenty seconds and claw his way down the mast from the crow's nest in another ten seconds flat.

'Rocks!' screamed Banzai.

Grubson stared at him.

'Straight ahead – ROCKS!' screamed Banzai again. 'I saw them through my telescope. I saw them – them great BIG ROCKS!' Banzai was pulling at Grubson's coat, trying to make him do something.

Still getting no reaction, Banzai grabbed onto his captain's coat collar and pulled Grubson towards him, eyeball to eyeball, and hissed into his face:

'Sailing instructions! Sailing instructions!'

Maybe it was the wide-eyed fear on Banzai's face, or perhaps it was the strong stink of garlic which brought Grubson to his senses but he suddenly seemed to remember that he was captain of The Beagle and jumped into action.

'Bring down the mainsail!' he ordered. 'Help me bring her about!'

Lefty and Sebastian obeyed Grubson at once, pulling

and tugging on the ropes attached to the biggest sail and fighting the wind to bring it down and under control. Meanwhile Banzai and Grubson hauled on the ship's wheel with all Grubson's weight and all Banzai's strength to try to turn The Beagle before they hit the rocks.

But none of them were quick enough...

MEANWHILE, BACK IN ST BENFRO...

Henri was standing at the top of eight flights of stairs outside the door of his friend, Horatio Fox. He had been soaked to the skin as he ran along the harbour wall and the climb up to the top flat of Gunfort Mansions had been a huge effort for the tiny dog.

His legs were trembling as he stood at the door, trying to get his breath back between terrible rasping wheezes. He pulled himself up as tall as he could stretch, reached out with one paw and just managed to grasp the bell-pull. Henri crumpled onto the floor as he heard the bell ding-a-linging somewhere far inside Horatio Fox's attic flat.

MEANWHILE, BACK ON BOARD THE BEAGLE...

The hold – was holed!

Lefty, Sebastian, Banzai, Grubson AND Marjorie were all bailing out The Beagle. They formed a chain from the hold, up the ladder, and onto the deck. Desperate to stop the seawater filling the ship, the dogs scooped water into big heavy buckets and passed them from paw to paw up to the cat at the top of the ladder, who then hurled the water overboard. There were times when Banzai's freakishly strong biceps were extremely useful on board a ship!

The gash where The Beagle had hit the rocks was big and letting in water faster than it could be bailed out.

'Face it!' squawked Marjorie. 'We're fighting a hopeless battle.'

Grubson didn't want to hear this. Frantically scooping water into buckets and swinging them up to Banzai, he asked her what she might suggest instead.

'Plug the hole – plug the hole!' Marjorie screeched.

Grubson, Lefty and Sebastian kept on bailing. Banzai kept on heaving heavy buckets overboard whilst Marjorie screamed over and over again, 'Plug the hole – plug the hole – plug the 'ole – plug the 'ole – plugtheoleplugtheoleplugtheole!'

'Let's try to plug the hole,' suggested Lefty.

'Good idea,' replied Grubson, 'with what?'

They stopped bailing and straightened their aching backs as they stared around the hold, seawater climbing up their legs, higher and higher as every minute passed.

MEANWHILE, BACK IN ST BENFRO . . .

Henri was sitting on a large antique couch, dwarfed by huge feather-filled velvet cushions. He felt warm and safe, sitting on a towel which Horatio had wrapped him in when he found his weeny Pug friend on his doorstep.

Henri was getting his breath back and the wheezing died down.

'Horatio – I need your help,' he whispered between sips of hot chocolate. Henri looked up at his friend seriously. 'I need the help of you and your special telescope!'

Horatio widened his eyes and raised his eyebrows. Henri was one of only two people who knew about his special telescope and he knew Henri would not ask for it unless it was very urgent.

The special telescope in question was inherited from Horatio's aunt – who had been a pirate. When she died, she had left everything to Horatio and "everything" had included her flat at the top of Gunfort Mansions which had a commanding view over the harbour and out to sea. Her special telescope was very large and stood in a turret which rose out through the ceiling of the flat and stuck out on top of the roof of the tall building. The circular turret had arched windows all the way round and the telescope lens could be poked out of any window to enable Horatio's aunt, or now Horatio or Henri, to see far away to the furthest horizons.

This was special enough, but what made this telescope very special was that it was a TALKING TELESCOPE! When Horatio put his eye to the telescope and looked through, it explained what he could see. At night, when Horatio aimed the lens to the skies, it would explain which stars and planets he could see – their names, how old they were, what kind of rock they were made of and how far from Earth they were.

During the day, when looking across the beach and the sea and the headland, it would tell him what kind of birds he could see, who the people were and what they were doing – and sometimes, why they were doing it!

Today, Henri needed to look through the telescope to see what had happened to The Beagle.

Henri jumped down from the couch and ran across to Horatio's huge chart chest (also inherited from his pirate aunt). He pulled open one of the wide shallow drawers and brought out the charts which showed the waters which stretched from St Benfro to France.

Henri had been looking closely at his father's charts after he had set off earlier in the month and he had seen where Grubson had pencilled in different routes. Henri had looked carefully at the charts and had seen where they pinpointed rocks or dangerous currents or hidden shallows. His days left alone in the house had not been wasted. He knew exactly how to read the tide tables and understand the maps.

He knew that the full moon was bringing a high tide and he had guessed that The Beagle would take the shortest (and most dangerous) way home. And there was a terrible storm. Henri shivered deep within the folds of the towel as he explained this to Horatio.

When he had finished, he turned his big watery eyes to the fox and wheezed, 'Please help me Horatio.'

'Right you are!' said the fox, jumping up from his chair. He picked up his aunt's pipe and jammed it between his lips, chewing on it as he concentrated. He didn't ever actually smoke the pipe – he was far too young to do that – but chewing on it helped him think!

Horatio stood at the bottom of the spiral staircase which led up to the telescope turret – he squinted at the chart and turned it to line up with his compass so that he knew exactly which window to open.

'Come on young Henri!' he said excitedly and, pausing only to frown at the barometer on the wall (which was pointing to STORM), they ran round and round the spiral staircase and up to the big talking telescope.

Up in the turret, the wind howled around the windows and rain whipped against the glass. The storm was getting nearer and stronger and if the barometer was to be believed, it would only get worse!

Horatio pulled on his big yellow sou'wester, then pushed his chosen window wide open and turned the telescope. By the time he had cranked the brass handle to extend the lens out into the air, both Horatio and Henri were soaked by the rain lashing in through the window.

Horatio put his eye to the telescope and scanned the horizon for any sign of a sail.

MEANWHILE, BACK ON BOARD THE BEAGLE...

Grubson and his crew had realised that things were worse than they had thought. Much worse. Bailing out was just not working. They also realised that The Beagle was sinking – which made them all feel a bit sick. And Grubson realised that Marjorie was right – which made him feel even sicker. But not as sick as Marjorie herself who was now flumped in the bottom of her wildly swinging cage, eyes closed. She had turned very green and was now just mumbling to herself.

'Plug the 'ole – plug the 'ole – plug the 'ole.'

Grubson stood in the hold of The Beagle, soaked to the bone, his fur sticking to him. He looked at the billowing dresses, now dipping in the salty water; the bicycle roped against the creaking timbers up to its saddle in seawater, the carpet bag (which Banzai had moved to a higher cubby hole and which was still dry) and the grand piano which was still in its crate but was now standing in water up to its keyboard.

As captain of The Beagle, Grubson had to save his ship and all her crew. His friends! So, pushing thoughts of a perfect Christmas to one side, Grubson shouted instructions as the wind ratcheted up another notch and threw The Beagle even higher off the tops of the waves.

'Plug the hole with the grand piano!' shouted

Grubson.

With that, quick as lightning, Lefty, Sebastian and Banzai set about freeing the grand piano from the crate. They didn't bother with knots or being careful, they tore the crate apart with axes and wrenched the piano out of its cosy little nest of calico and sawdust. Then they all leaned together and began to heave the grand piano across the hold towards the hole which was still gushing in water.

MEANWHILE, BACK IN ST BENFRO . . .

Horatio's talking telescope had become very excited – Horatio and Henri listened, holding their breath.

'The Beagle is just off Monastery Island – listing to starboard – no sign of any crew on deck!'

Henri jumped up next to the fox and pushed his head between Horatio's face and the telescope. Closing one eye, he looked through the long tube and out to sea. At first everything looked fuzzy and twitchy, but when he held his breath and tried harder, he could clearly see The Beagle – jumping and rolling, pitching and crashing on the dark stormy waters.

'The Beagle is beginning to level out,' said the telescope, 'it is definitely better balanced and I can see buckets of water shooting from the hatch.' Henri whimpered a bit and put his eye back to the lens again.

As he did so, The Beagle seemed to be walloped straight from the top of one gigantic wave to another, thudding and jolting as she went.

'The sails are ripping!' shouted Henri and the telescope.

MEANWHILE, BACK ON BOARD THE BEAGLE . . .

The grand piano had slotted into the hole perfectly. Wedged keyboard-first through the gap, lid open, it securely plugged the hole and the seawater stopped gushing in.

With no time to lose, Lefty, Sebastian, Banzai and Grubson set to work with the buckets again – filling bucket after bucket and throwing the water out through the hatch. Gradually the water subsided until it was only sloshing around their ankles. Exhausted, they fell in a big soggy heap and panted. The only sounds were the creaking ship's timbers, the howling of the storm and a strange watery plinky-plonky sound as the sea rippled across the keyboard underneath The Beagle and played an eerie little tune. . .

Gasping to get their breath back, the crew were thankful for a moment's rest. Until they heard a deafening roar and a ripping noise as two of The Beagle's biggest sails tore straight across the middle as the ship was sent bouncing and juddering from the crest of one wave to the next.

Sebastian ran up onto the deck and gasped when he saw his magnificent white sails hanging in tatters from the main mast. All his stitching, all his careful seam-strengthening had not managed to outlast the storm.

'Now what?' asked Lefty, looking from Grubson to Sebastian and from Sebastian to Banzai.

MEANWHILE, BACK IN ST BENFRO . . .

Horatio couldn't quite believe his eyes, but he could believe his talking telescope.

'The crew, which is a French Pug, a Mongrel, a well-bred Spaniel and a Siamese cat have appeared on deck.'

Henri wheezed with relief.

'They seem to be getting dressed up for a party!' exclaimed the telescope. Horatio and Henri looked at one another.

'Ah no! My mistake – the cat has run up to the top of the mast carrying a very pretty pink dress. The Mongrel is at half-mast with another very pretty dress – a blue one, with bows on it. They are tying the dresses to the mast and throwing the old sails overboard!'

The telescope went quiet.

'What are they doing now?' asked Henri breathlessly. 'What now?'

'They seem to be hanging lots of dresses from the mast,' said Horatio.

'And throwing everything else overboard!' finished the telescope.

Henri popped his head up again, squinted and saw his father's ship, now nice and straight again, festooned with party dresses which billowed out from the masts like the prettiest, sparkliest, laciest sails in the world. The Beagle looks beautiful – and very Christmassy, thought Henri.

Then he noticed barrels and crates, pots and pans, piles of old sails, bottles of rum, nets of oranges and a huge hamper of cheese being thrown overboard! All the crew seemed determined to throw everything into the sea. They worked as a perfect team until suddenly Banzai appeared to jump onto Grubson's head, grab a very large carpet bag from Grubson's clutches and run up the mast – all the way to the crow's nest, where he stuffed the bag.

Grubson was shouting at Banzai, but Henri couldn't hear anything above the sound of the driving rain, the crashing waves and the shrieking wind.

The telescope knew exactly what Grubson had shouted, but it didn't think it was suitable to repeat to Henri's young ears.

MEANWHILE, BACK ON BOARD THE BEAGLE . . .

Marjorie was feeling a lot better. She flew up onto the deck and then up to the crow's nest, or the Parrot Perch, as she preferred to call it.

She got Banzai's telescope out of the carpet bag (he was too busy throwing things overboard to notice) and had a look through.

'Land ahoy – land ahoy!' she squawked.

Lefty, Sebastian and Banzai stopped what they were doing and cheered – doing a little dance on the deck.

They came to a sudden stop when they saw Grubson's face. He was standing at the helm holding half the ship's wheel in one paw and the other half – in the other paw. The Beagle's wheel had split clean in two! Looking up at his parrot, Grubson said quietly, 'I know you can see land Marjorie, but how can I steer us there without a wheel?'

Now at the mercy of the wind, The Beagle was being tossed on the wave-tops, unable to steer her own path through the heaving seas.

'Row?' said Banzai, already shaking his head at his own hopeless suggestion as he clung to the mast.

'Swim?' said Lefty.

'Don't be so silly!' spluttered Banzai as he skidded across the tilting deck.

'I've got it!' burst out Sebastian, shouting to make himself heard above the wind. 'I didn't have the heart to throw Fabrice's new bicycle overboard, even though you ordered us to jettison everything. I'm sorry about that, Captain . . .' He paused, trying to work out what Grubson's raised eyebrows meant.

'Perhaps,' he continued, 'if we lash the two bicycle wheels together they may just make a helm strong enough to steer us home?' his voice faded away again. Grubson's eyebrows were still raised.

There was a sudden and frenzied dash for the hatch door. Banzai squeezed through first and reappeared moments later with the bicycle wheels.

Lefty tied them together using his strongest knots and Sebastian nailed them to the stub of wood left by the old wheel. Standing back proudly, the crew made way for their captain to take the helm and steer them home.

Trying not to think about what Frank Aquitaine would say if he could see what they had done with his beautiful bicycle, Grubson stood behind his strange and shiny-spoked helm and gave instructions.

'Full sail ahead with the ball gowns!'

Marjorie flew back up to the crow's nest to point the way home.

'Land ahoy!' she squawked again and this time, Lefty, Sebastian, Banzai AND Grubson stopped what they were doing and cheered – doing a little dance on the deck.

Meanwhile, Marjorie peered more closely through Banzai's telescope, scanning the beach and the harbour and the rooftops of St Benfro – and stopped when she came eyeball to eyeball with a very worried looking Henri!

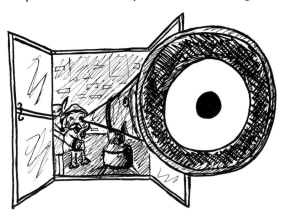

MEANWHILE, BACK IN ST BENFRO . . .

'Aaahhhhhhh!' squealed Henri – he had been watching Grubson and his crew dancing on the deck of The Beagle when he had suddenly come telescope to telescope with Marjorie.

She was squinting and frowning STRAIGHT AT HIM!

'GIANT PARROT!' shouted the telescope. 'Take cover – take cover! GIANT PARROT!'

But Horatio and Henri were not listening – they were running back down, round and round the spiral staircase and running all the way down eight flights of stairs and out into the rain.

By now the harbour wall and the beach were lined with crowds – all anxiously watching The Beagle in full sail – dresses ballooning in the wind and the sound of a piano accompanying the crash of the sea. Leaning into the wind, eyes blinking into the driving rain, the townsfolk of St Benfro were shouting and calling to The Beagle and crew – urging them on through the storm.

Mrs Grubson and her family were at the front of the crowds. Fabrice was jumping up and down watching the tug-boat captain prepare to pull The Beagle to safety when she made it into the calm waters of the harbour. Clementina was clinging to her mother, both of them trying to make out the shape of Grubson on the deck. Clementina thought she could hear a piano playing a most beautiful and eerie tune – or was it the wind playing tricks on her ears?

And Bella? Instead of strutting about with her snub nose in the air, thinking of nasty things to say about her friends, she was calling and shouting to The Beagle. She wasn't pulling a face or scowling and she wasn't fussing about the bow in her hair (which was soaked and totally flattened). And she wasn't showing off! She was wet through, clumps of her fur were sticking out at odd angles and her big eyes were full of hope for Grubson's safe return. When The Beagle finally made it to the harbour, she laughed and danced and smiled and hugged anyone she knew – and some people she didn't know! When she was finally able to run up the gangplank and jump into Grubson's arms and cover him in kisses, Grubson thought she had never looked prettier.

And what about Henri? Henri stumbled along the harbour wall as fast as his tired little legs could carry him. Swamped in the yellow sou'wester, no one recognised him until he crawled to the front of the crowd between everyone's legs, scrabbled along the gangplank and wheezed.

'Welcome home for Christmas, Papa!'

Grubson Pug's Christmas Voyage

The Storm

Grubson Pug's Christmas Voyage

Chapter Ten

Christmas Day

Christmas Day dawned bright and sunny in St Benfro. The storm had passed during the night and the sea was once more blue and well-behaved. The Christmas bells from St Benfro church rang out through the cobbled streets and the frost sparkled on the rooftops.

Inside the Grubson house, a huge fire was crackling in the grate and the Christmas tree stood at the window, festooned with strings of gold-painted shells and glittering in the light of tiny candles pinned to the branches.

There were not many parcels under the tree, but nobody minded. Clementina was playing the old piano – crashing out a few carols and Bella was laughing as she played blind-man's bluff with her brothers.

Grubson was looking out of his window at The Beagle thinking about his travels and the stormy voyage home. He sighed, wishing he hadn't lost all the presents, but he was relieved that The Beagle and all her crew had got home safely. Adele came in from the kitchen – a big waft of turkey, chestnuts and Christmas pudding trailing behind her. Smiling proudly at her husband, she brought him a mince pie and stroked his ears.

'When I thought you might be lost at sea,' she said, 'and when I thought we might never see you again, I realised how much I would miss you. You tried so hard to please all the children and that led you into terrible danger. I love you very much Grubson.'

Grubson was so happy to hear this that he danced his wife right round the house until stopping underneath the mistletoe nose to nose.

He thought about the little golden brooch and wished he hadn't lost it. He had a vague recollection of putting it somewhere safe but after all the frantic activity of trying to save The Beagle, he couldn't remember what he had done with it.

That Christmas Night, Grubson sat in his favourite chair by the fireside. Henri sat on his lap (singeing his little knees which were dangling slightly too close to the fire) listening to his stories. Grubson had a story for each of his children: Fraulein Schneerer's story for Clementina; the story from Frank Aquitaine for Fabrice; Senor Castanet's tale for Bella and Grubson's own story of the voyage home for Henri.

Afterword

Whilst Grubson was telling his Christmas stories to his family, outside, in the darkness, Banzai was up in the crow's nest of The Beagle. The rest of the crew had gone on shore to visit friends and family. Banzai was enjoying having the run of The Beagle all to himself. No one was about in the harbour and he was quite alone as he sat up high, whistling Christmas carols and sea shanties and rootling about in his carpet bag.

Everything seemed to be there – including his telescope.

Suddenly he noticed something he had not personally put there!

A little golden ship with a diamond at the top of the mast.

Banzai stopped whistling, puzzled. He couldn't think when or who or how the brooch had got into his carpet bag.

He guessed it was very precious and he knew someone, somewhere would want it back one day. So he decided to look after the little golden ship until he could think of a way to return it – or until the mystery owner came to claim it back.

After a while, he tucked it safely back into his bag and sat looking at the stars through his telescope.

And that is where we should leave Banzai for the time being – the story of how he returned the brooch and what it is he keeps locked away in his carpet bag will have to wait until another time.

Until then, I wish you a very merry Christmas!

Captain John Selby

THE END

Afterword

Thank you!

Thank you Max – for pointing out Grubson Pug when we were on a voyage to St Malo! Who would've guessed he'd have such stories to tell?

Thank you – to my friends who pecked me to do this (you know who you are) and my family; Minnie, Tony and Helen for all your encouragement and good sense.

Thank you to my wonderful 'boyses' – Sam, Tom and Joel for the nights of laughter and naughtiness and epic story-telling during your childhood, when you should have been asleep!

And thank you David – for your love, for your kind heart and your unswerving belief in me. Right back at you sweetheart!

And not forgetting you. Thank YOU – for reading this book!